P9-BZO-146
our generation®
This is Jenny's story.

JENNY™

THE SWEET SHOPPE MYSTERY

BY

SUSAN CAPPADONIA LOVE

COVER ART BY KRISTI VALIANT
STORY ILLUSTRATIONS BY TRISH ROUELLE

An Our Generation® *book*
MAISON JOSEPH BATTAT LTD *Publisher*

A very special thanks to the editor,
Joanne Burke Casey.

ISBN: 978-0-9883165-5-3
Printed in China

To Peach, who cooked up the idea for this tale, and Sophie, cake decorator extraordinaire

Read all the adventures in the
Our Generation® Book Series

One Smart Cookie
featuring Hally™

Blizzard on Moose Mountain
featuring Katelyn™

Stars in Your Eyes
featuring Sydney Lee™

The Note in the Piano
featuring Mary Lyn™

The Mystery of the Vanishing Coin
featuring Eva®

Adventures at Shelby Stables
featuring Lily Anna®

The Sweet Shoppe Mystery
featuring Jenny™

The Jumpstart Squad
featuring Juliet™

The Dress in the Window
featuring Audrey-Ann®

The Jukebox Babysitters
featuring Ashley-Rose®

In the Limelight
featuring Evelyn®

The Most Fantabulous Pajama Party Ever
featuring Willow™

Magic Under the Stars
featuring Shannon™

The Circus and the Secret Code
featuring Alice™

Read more about **Our Generation®** books and dolls online:
www.ogdolls.com

CONTENTS

EXTRA! EXTRA! READ ALL ABOUT IT!

Big words, wacky words, powerful words, funny words...
*what do they all mean? They are marked with this symbol * .*
Look them up in the Glossary at the end of this book.

Chapter One

THE QUEEN OF CAKES

What does a chocolate cake have to do with a volcano? I found out at cake decorating class when my cousin Lucy asked me a question that was tricky to answer.

"How do I like the cake you made?" I stalled for time. "Well, it's…it's so…*wow.*" Finding the right words to describe her so-called cake was important because this was Lucy's fifth baking failure in a row. I didn't want to hurt her feelings.

I clasped my hands, put my two pointer fingers together and tapped my chin. Words popped into my head that were just right. Not a lie and not unkind either. "It's *really something*!" I exclaimed.

"Thanks," Lucy said, beaming with pride. "It's hot out of the oven."

Just then a woman dressed in a bright white baker's uniform and neck scarf bustled into the room. She stopped in her tracks right in front of Lucy's "creation," which looked like a giant mountain of chocolate cake. She covered her mouth with a cupped hand, but her smile was creeping across her whole face. Her eyes twinkled with amusement.

This woman has won many awards for her amazing cakes—and some of them were as tall as me! She's a master chef and baker, and she's been our cake decorating teacher for more than five weeks now. The embroidery on the chest of her uniform says "Edna Bea" but lots of people call her Queen Bea, a nickname that stuck after her latest cookbook, *The Queen of Cakes*, sold over a million copies.

For years, people have been pestering her for a secret cake recipe she has. She says that, because it was her mom's recipe, it isn't hers to give out.

Queen Bea glanced at Lucy's cake again. Holding back a laugh, she said, "That is a very creative approach to this week's homework assignment." Lucy took that as a compliment*. She grinned from ear to ear, like

she'd just won a ticket to Water Planet Theme Park.

I felt happy for Lucy. Finally she felt like a success at baking.

Every week Queen Bea gave us a homework assignment to bake a cake and decorate it using the techniques we learned in class. And every week Lucy's cakes turned out somewhat unusual.

The first one came in five separate pieces, which is to say it had fallen apart. That was no problem for Lucy, though. She drizzled the chunks with white icing*, plunked a plastic penguin on one and said they were iceberg cakes.

The next week Lucy brought a cake that was completely sunken in the middle, like a basketball had been dribbled on the center. Three batches of frosting couldn't fill in the crater.

Her third cake was shriveled up, burned to a crisp and the frosting flowers were wobbly. It looked like she had decorated it while riding down a bumpy road.

No one ever saw Lucy's fourth cake. She said it was so slippery (*a slippery cake?*), it slid right off the plate and splashed (*splashed?*) onto her driveway when she was coming to class.

As bad as her fifth cake was, it was actually an improvement over the others.

"I can't wait for everyone to try it," Lucy said to me. "You know how yours are always light and fluffy and delicious? Well, I did just what you said to

do: I beat the batter for twenty minutes."

I bit my lip. "Two minutes, Lucy, not 20," I said softly.

"Ohhh..." Her voice trailed off and she looked slightly concerned. Instantly she brightened right up. "Not to worry. I still think it's my best cake yet."

"You call that a cake?!" chimed in my four-and-a-half-year-old sister Sadie. She was there with my mom dropping me off at class.

Val, a cake decorating student who also goes to Little Falls Elementary School with me, laughed out loud at my sister's reaction.

Sadie didn't catch the warning look from my mom. She was happily parading her tiny plastic animals around all the cakes on the counter. There were two of each kind of animal and she carried them in an ark*-shaped case everywhere she went.

"Cakes have frosting," demanded Sadie. "Where's the frosting?"

"That's a funny story," Lucy answered. "I frosted the cake, baked it, took it out of the oven and the frosting had just disappeared."

Hold on, I thought, *did Lucy just say she frosted the cake before she baked it?*

I scanned the eight cakes that lined the baking counter at The Sweet Shoppe, the candy and coffee shop where we met for class. Behind each cake stood the student who made it.

First there was Professor Lynn. Her cake was shaped like an open book with "pages" made out of frosted cake slices and a gummy "bookworm" wearing eyeglasses made from string licorice. She was clearly puzzled by the sight of Lucy's cake.

Next to her was her husband Ken, whose cake was a skyscraper with tiny windows outlined in frosting and solar panels* made out of chocolate bars. His cakes looked just like the buildings he designed (when he's not baking, he's an architect). He frowned at Lucy's mountain and his face said it all: "What in the world is that?"

Then came the train engineer, Mr. Hiro. His cakes were always shaped like trains. The first week he made a red locomotive*, then a boxcar, a passenger car, a coal car and the last one was a caboose. Mr.

Hiro wasn't paying a bit of attention to Lucy's cake because he was asking Queen Bea for her secret cake recipe (for the third time!).

Next to him was Karlin, owner of the Rock & Roll Bowling Alley. He started a baking business on the side so customers could buy cakes for bowling parties. His cake was half round and covered with deep blue frosting and sparkling blue sugar crystals. It had three holes for fingers just like a bowling ball. He was shaking his head in wonder at Lucy's cake.

Beside him was Kathleen. Her cake was a cute bunny covered in coconut, with pink frosted ears and a pink nose made out of a candy heart.

After that was Val, who made a rainbow cake with gold-covered chocolate coins sprinkled on the bottom. I had to admit it was cute, but I felt miffed that she had laughed at Lucy's cake.

Then came Lucy with her gigantic hill of a cake.

I was at the very end of the counter with the purple cake I made. It was three stories high and decorated with green and purple starbursts, lilac daisies and a purple rose on top.

"Jenny, your cakes always look like they came right out of a magazine," Lucy gushed. "Will you show me how to make a rose like that sometime?"

"Sure," I told her, happy we could spend time together and bake, too.

Then my smile turned into a gasp. I noticed something moving inside Lucy's cake. I jumped back from the baking counter. "Uh, Lucy, I think your cake is…erupting!"

Chapter Two

CAKES, CAKES, ALL OVER THE PLACE

Lucy's cake was bubbling over in a most alarming way.

"Oh, goodness," Queen Bea croaked, "if I didn't know better, I'd say there's lava coming out of the top of your mountain—er, I mean your cake."

"Lava? I like that idea," Lucy said, nodding her head. "I'll call this week's baking assignment 'Vesuvius,' named after the volcano in Italy. But you can eat *this* lava, because it's delicious fudge frosting."

The students stared at it in amazement.

Queen Bea quickly changed the subject. "Well class, thank you to everyone who donated their cakes and cupcakes to the bake sale at the Daisy Brook Animal Shelter last weekend. And a special thanks to Jenny, who brought 24 bumblebee cupcakes. Every single one sold in the first ten minutes and people

were coming back for more.

"Okay, let's get started discussing our homework assignments this week."

Sadie scooped her tiny animals into the ark carrying case. Even though she'd be back in one hour to pick me up, she hugged me and hung on tight as if she couldn't bear to be apart. *My sweetie pie*, I thought.

"Remember," continued Queen Bea, "we're grading our cakes on style and imagination."

Mom took Sadie's hand and led her to the door. As Sadie exited, we all heard her loud and clear, "I think somebody will be getting a big fat E for Explosion."

Val giggled. Mr. Hiro let out a loud "Ha!" And chuckles could be heard around the room.

I noticed Lucy's shoulders slump and her smile fade.

That kid, I thought. *So lovable one minute, and yet so irritating the next!*

"Don't listen to her," I whispered to Lucy, "I'm sure you'll get an A+ for Aroma*. It smells delicious."

Lucy's sunny mood was spoiled. It bothered her that she just couldn't get the hang of baking. I could

tell she was down in the dumps for the rest of the class. And that's just not like her.

One thing about my cousin Lucy is that she's positively positive—all the time. That's one of the reasons she's also my best friend. She's bubbly, fun and has a way of looking on the bright side of everything.

For example, it poured last year at her Birthday Picnic Party. The sandwiches turned to soggy mush and a powerful wind swept in and carried all her balloons off into the sky. Did the downpour ruin her party? No way. She twirled and danced in the rain, just tickled* pink that she could wear the blue polka-dotted rain boots she'd received as a birthday present.

And once when I complained about our English teacher giving us an extra writing assignment, Lucy turned it into something good. She excitedly squeaked, "Jenny, write about when you went to the Daisy Brook Animal Shelter to pick out a cat. Remember? Instead of you picking out a cat, a certain cat pranced right up and *picked you*."

She was talking about Snuggles, my adopted cat. I just love that funny guy with all my heart. Petting him is my number one favorite thing to do.

Snuggles lies on his back with all four legs up in the air and he's quite a sight. As long as I scratch him behind the ears or under his chin, he'll listen to me pour my heart out all night long.

When I told him that I got picked last for dodge ball, or that I forgot my homework and got in

trouble, or that Sadie put a dill pickle in my lunchbox (not wrapped) and it stunk up the whole classroom, Snuggles half-shut his eyes and purred. It was as if he were saying, "Relax. Look at me. Am I worried? Of course not, because everything will be okay."

My second favorite thing to do was my new hobby: decorating cakes and cupcakes. Once I got started on this new adventure, there was no stopping me.

I thought about cake ideas the second I woke up in the morning. I daydreamed about decorating while I was sitting on the bus and when I was supposed to be paying attention in class. And as soon as I got home from soccer practice, I grabbed my sketchpad and colored pencils, sprawled* out on my bed and drew cakes I'd dreamed up earlier that day.

When it was past my bedtime I doodled under my covers with a flashlight. Soon I'd hear a muffled mom-voice say, "Top-secret cake decorating, huh? Well maybe two more minutes, then it's flashlights out, okay?"

Good ideas popped up at unexpected times so the sketchpad was always with me. I also used it to jot down notes about colors, candy sprinkles, decorations, sizes, shapes, frosting flavors and pretty much all things yummy.

My baking assistant (my mom) kept the pantry stocked with all the baking supplies we needed. That way we could try out a new design whenever an idea came to me. We'd made everything I'd ever sketched—that was a lot of baked goods!

But there was one problem: all that baking created more cakes and cupcakes than our family could ever eat. I put them in the freezer until not another cupcake could fit. Then I dropped them off at my neighbors', brought them to parties or to my grandma's senior* center.

"Orders" for baked goods began trickling in from people we knew who had tasted my creations and wanted a cake for a birthday party, baby shower or other special occasions.

People insisted on paying me, but I felt a little funny taking money from friends and family. So I came up with a plan that everybody felt good about: a $5 fee per dozen* cupcakes covered the ingredients, and whatever money was leftover would be donated to the Daisy Brook Animal Shelter. People seemed to like that idea because everyone knew the shelter badly needed a larger building.

Here's why: when a factory* closed here in Little Falls more than a thousand people lost their jobs and could no longer afford to take good care of their pets. So lots of cats, dogs, guinea pigs and rabbits

ended up at the shelter to be adopted. The animal shelter needed more room to make all the animals feel comfortable until they found families to love them.

I discovered a cute cookie jar in the basement that was shaped like a fluffy kitty wearing a yellow bow. My mom said I could use it to hold the money we made for the animal shelter. We named it the "Coins for a Cause" Jar. Quarters, dimes, nickels and pennies already covered the bottom.

❧ ❧

The last twenty minutes of cake decorating class were always delicious because after we discussed baking and frosting, we got to taste each other's cakes.

Everyone uses the same recipe, but each cake tastes a little different. This can happen for a few reasons. The burners in an oven might not heat evenly (so the cake burns in the back but is golden brown in the front). Or the ingredients that go into a cake don't always taste the same, so the cakes don't taste exactly alike. For example, the vanilla that my mom bought might taste sweeter or stronger than another bottle of

vanilla.

Mr. Hiro's caboose cake, Karlin's bowling ball, Lynn's open book and bookworm, Ken's skyscraper, Val's rainbow, Kathleen's bunny, and my triple layer cake all tasted scrumptious. But as might be expected when batter is beaten for 20 minutes, the volcano was as hard as a rock. Queen Bea broke a sweat trying to chip away at the lava.

"Mmmn-mmm!" I smacked my lips loudly, and rolled a large chunk of lava around in my mouth. I wondered if it would ever melt or even become chewy.

While Lucy talked to Karlin about a Bowl-A-Thon she wanted to organize for our class, Queen Bea took me aside.

She put her hand gently on my shoulder and said in a hushed voice, "Can you please stay for few minutes after class tonight? There's something I'd like to discuss with you, but I don't want to hurt Lucy's feelings."

She looked nervously in Lucy's direction.

Poor Lucy, I thought, *is she getting kicked out of cake decorating class?*

Chapter Three

CUPCAKE CORNER

Lucy opened the door of The Sweet Shoppe for her dad. "See you at the bus stop in the morning, Jenny," she said.

"Bye, Uncle Bob," I called out. He managed a smile, but his face was strained and red from carrying the heavy Vesuvius cake. The door clanged shut. Lucy waved to me as she walked past the window, then to my mom and Sadie who were there to pick me up.

I felt like I was going to burst. If Lucy got the boot* from class, she'd feel like a total loser.

"Please don't kick Lucy out of class," I blurted. "We'll work together. She'll improve, you'll see—"

Queen Bea gave a huge snort. "What? Goodness no. I love that kid's spirit. She just keeps trying and that's more important than creating a perfect cake. She has a cheerful attitude and I really admire Lucy for that.

"I have *good* news to tell you. But I didn't want to say it in front of Lucy because I thought I'd run it by you first."

Phew! I thought.

"Here's the thing. Soon I'm leaving for the vacation of my dreams. I'll be staying at my son's cabin in the wilderness* for a month where I'll work on my new cookbook, *Cooking Around the Campfire: S'Mores & More*. There will be no phone, no computer, no cars, no electricity—just nature, gardening, chopping wood and baking over a campfire. Sounds heavenly, right?"

Not really, I thought, and I guess I might have made a face because Queen Bea read my mind.

She grinned. "Well, it does to me. But anyway, as you know my cupcakes and cakes are sold here at The Sweet Shoppe. And since I'm not going to be here for awhile, I suggested that you fill in for me. Your baking really seems to be catching on in Little Falls. And Mr. Figg, the owner of The Sweet Shoppe, likes the idea that the profits will go to the Daisy Brook Animal Shelter."

"Wow!" I shouted.

"That's fantastic," my mom said.

Sadie clapped and jumped up and down. "I can help. I'm a big kid now."

"Maybe in a few years, Sadie," said my mom, winking at me. It's a family joke that on Sadie's birthday, she thought she turned fourteen instead of four.

Queen Bea's
treats sold out
today. Please stop
by tomorrow.

Queen Bea pointed to an old-fashioned, bright blue cabinet in the corner of The Sweet Shoppe. It had shelves on the top and a cupboard down below with doors.

"Starting next Thursday," she said, "that's your cabinet to display your fancy, funny, pretty, colorful—and most of all delicious—desserts."

"I think I'll call it Cupcake Corner," I decided.

"Good," said Queen Bea. Then she hesitated*. "I have an idea for Lucy, too. I've noticed that although her baking skills still need improvement, she's enthusiastic and terrific with organizing projects. It's a lot of work running your own business. Maybe you could use the help of a partner?"

"Do you mean help with things like keeping track of orders and making deliveries?" I asked.

"Exactly," Queen Bea agreed. "You two would be a good team. But if she does help out in the kitchen, make sure she frosts the cakes *after* she bakes them!" That made us all burst out laughing.

"Thank you for giving us this chance," I told her.

"My pleasure, darlin'," she said. "It's easy to believe in people who are creative and practice, practice, practice! I also believe in the good work you're doing for the animal shelter."

❧ ❧

I called Lucy the minute I got home to tell her the wonderful news: starting Cupcake Corner, the new way to raise money for the shelter, and Queen Bea recommending us as partners.

We made a deal: I would be in charge of the creative side of the business (designs and baking) and Lucy would be in charge of the business end (which included everything else).

"I'll start making posters tonight!" she said. "There's a large party for my mom's company at Deb's Diner in two weeks. I'll call to see if they need a cake. How about if we offer customers at The Sweet Shoppe a 'buy five dozen cupcakes, get one dozen free' deal? What if I...."

Lucy had one idea after another. She said she'd better get off the phone and get going on plans for Cupcake Corner.

❧ ❧

Between soccer practice, schoolwork, homework for cake decorating class and getting Cupcake Corner up and running, life was busy busy busy.

Lucy went full-speed ahead putting up yellow posters

all over town. The beauty salon, coffee shop, hardware store and pharmacy all displayed her posters in their front window. They read:

DELICIOUS JUST GOT BETTER
AT CUPCAKE CORNER
Buy creative cakes and cupcakes
at The Sweet Shoppe today
or place your order for a party.

Our first official Cupcake Corner order was from Val's mom. After class one night she told me that she was throwing a Painting Party. Her friends were coming over to help her paint the kitchen hot pink.

Val's mom said she sent out hot pink invitations, the guests would wear pink, the food would be pink and the decorations would be pink. She said Val couldn't make the cupcakes because she was going to her friend's cottage that weekend.

"I saw your posters," she said. "Can I please place an order for 24 pink cupcakes with pink frosting?"

Val spun around so her back was to me and walked over to the window. Was she angry? Jealous? Both?

Jenny
TO
MOMMY
SADIE

I jumped right into making our new bakery "business" a success and so did Lucy.

She wrote special orders on the calendar and put grocery lists together for ingredients we needed for the coming week. She kept track of how much we spent. And she delivered desserts to The Sweet Shoppe.

My baking days were Saturday afternoon (our biggest delivery to The Sweet Shoppe was on Sunday morning) and Wednesday after school (because there was no soccer practice on that day). There were cupcakes and cakes everywhere in my house on those days.

And when I wasn't actually in the kitchen baking, I was coming up with new designs. It started taking over my life.

❧ ❧

One Wednesday in geography class, my teacher called on me. "Jenny, please tell the class the names of the Great Lakes."

I looked up from my cake decorating sketchpad

and answered, "Very Vanilla, Double* Chocolate, Cherrylicious, Pumpkin Spice and Peppermint Swirl."

"That's what I thought," she said unhappily. "Last week when I asked you to name the states in New England, you said, 'Gingerbread, Fudge Marble, Lemon Supreme, Angel Food and Maple Walnut.'"

A row over and one seat back, I heard Val sniff loudly. *Miss Perfect*, I thought.

My teacher told me it was high time to get my head out of the clouds, or in this case, out of the cake batter! And then she said what no student wants to hear.

"I think you'd better go spend the rest of class with Principal Adams. And Jenny? Leave the sketchpad here."

❧ ❧

When I returned from the principal's office, all the kids were gone. And so was my sketchpad!

I asked my teacher if she knew where it was.

She didn't, but she didn't seem too upset that it was missing. It was recess, so I ran outside to the playground. Nobody there remembered seeing it either.

Crushed. That's how I felt. All my ideas were in that sketchpad.

Where could it be? Did someone take it? Who would want a whole bunch of cake doodles?

Chapter Four
TWICE AS MICE

That night was baking night, so while we were mixing and measuring ingredients, I told my mom the day's events: not concentrating in class, going to Principal Adams' office and the missing sketchpad.

Sadie was tossing her little plastic animals into the air and trying to teach herself how to juggle. They were dropping left and right, and all over the place.

"Glad I hid the apples," Mom joked. "They'd be applesauce by now."

When I went to get the baking pans out of the cupboard, a skunk fell on my head. I handed it to Sadie and opened the doors. There, tied with a yellow bow, was a brand new drawing pad. On the front in purple marker was written "Sketchpad #2." Mom had talked with the principal earlier and knew

all about what had happened.

"Thanks, Mom," I said.

"You're welcome." She smiled, then frowned. "I want this cake decorating fundraising* to work out. But if you're so distracted that you can't pay attention in class, I'm afraid you're going to have to close Cupcake Corner."

"But Mom, figuring out how to make a crocodile cake is so much more interesting than reading, geography and math."

"I see what you're saying," she said. "Let's make a double batch of this chocolate cake mix."

"OK," I said, and began to measure all the ingredients.

"Wait a second," my mom said. "How did you know how to double all the ingredients?"

"Easy. The recipe called for two cups of sugar so I added two plus two, which equals four. Four cups."

"Aha!" she smiled. "Good thing you know math. That sure makes it a lot easier to measure.

Now how will you find a recipe for a crocodile cake?"

"I'll look it up, which means it sure is a good thing I know how to read."

It was easy to see where she was going with this line of thought. We came to an agreement. I would only use Sketchpad #2 on the bus, at recess, lunch and after all my homework was done. No ifs, ands or buts. That way I wouldn't be doodling when I wasn't supposed to be.

❧ ❧

Word was spreading about Cupcake Corner and sales were better than expected. Tango Mango Cake, Midnight Snack Cupcakes, Hunny Bunny Cake and Go Bananas Cake all flew off the shelves. The top seller was Strawberry Chocolate Chip Cupcakes followed by Zucchini Chocolate Cake (yum!).

There were a couple of treats that bombed, too. Pickles-and-Jam Muffins and Pucker Up Chocolate-Covered Pretzels weren't popular picks in Little Falls.

When Mr. Figg gave Lucy the money that was made at Cupcake Corner, Lucy would put the cash

and coins into two piles. One pile was the money we owed my mom for the ingredients that week. Whatever was left over was profit* and went into the "Coins for a Cause" Jar.

I had come up with a contest for the kids in my school to give us recipes that were a hit in their families. The recipe that was chosen would be made for Cupcake Corner and the winner got a prize—a dozen cupcakes. My business partner made a flier to put the word out to our classmates.

They warmed up to the idea right away and started giving us their recipes. One day we sat on my porch steps and leafed through the recipes that we'd collected in a purple sneaker box.

Lots of them were family favorites and had names like Grandma's Chocolate Cake, Aunt Lillian's Blueberry Cobbler or Mom's Mile-High Rhubarb Pie.

Some of them had five stars penciled on them or hand-written notes like "melts in your mouth!" and "sensational!"

"Listen to this one," Lucy said, scanning a green slip of paper. "Bubble Gum Cake with Cotton Candy Frosting."

"Yum," we both said together.

"That would be popular with the kids who come to The Sweet Shoppe," Lucy said. "How about this one? Potato Chip-and-Dip Cake. Hmnn, interesting."

"Hey, I have an idea. What if we made a school cookbook with all these recipes?" I asked.

"I love it!" Lucy said. "We could sell the cookbooks at Cupcake Corner and at school, then donate the

money to the animal shelter."

We couldn't wait to put our plan in motion.

"Let's jot down a list of what needs to be done," I suggested.

Cookbook To-do List:

1. Set a date for The Baking Bonanza* (that's when we'll bake and test all the recipes to make sure the measurements are correct and the cakes turn out just right).
2. Plan book sections (for example, Cakes & Cupcakes, Breads & Muffins, Pies & Tarts, Cookies & Brownies and Allergy-Free* Desserts).
3. Ask for volunteers and organize them into baking teams.
4. Find one large kitchen to do some of the baking and another large kitchen to make the allergy-free desserts.
5. Ask the grocery store if they'll donate ingredients.
6. Ask Lucy's mom if she'll type recipes into the computer so they can be sent to the printer*.
7. Get written permission from each person to use his or her recipe in the cookbook.

Right away, Lucy handed out fliers about the cookbook and got people interested. I'm shy when it comes to asking people to help out, but she's a pro. Even more recipes started pouring in and soon our purple box was full.

❧ ❧

I was ten minutes late to the last cake decorating class. Right before we left the house Sadie started crying and carrying on about her plastic animals. "Mr. and Mrs. Mouse are gone gone gone!" We looked under the sofa, shook out her blankets and even sifted through the sandbox.

"They'll turn up," my mom said. "I'm sure of it." We finally calmed Sadie down and headed for The Sweet Shoppe.

I felt a little blue* because class had been so much fun and now it was ending. But, instead of being sad, it turned out to be a big party.

Queen Bea decorated The Sweet Shoppe with streamers, party plates and cups that said "Congratulations" and gave us each a diploma*

that said we'd graduated from the Queen Bea School of Cake Decorating. Then she gave us each a bumper sticker that read, "Change the World, One Cake at a Time."

The feast was, of course, cake.

There was a map of the United States cake by Professor Lynn, a palace with a moat around it by Ken, an antique steam engine by Mr. Hiro, a long bowling alley with a ball rolling down to the ten pins at the end by Karlin, a white bathtub with two floating rubber duckies by Kathleen, a dog and doghouse by Val, a sailboat on a lake that sloped greatly to one side by Lucy, and a man-in-the-moon by me.

I tensed up as the boat on Lucy's cake started tipping...tipping more...then...plunk! It sank into a pool of blue icing. Lucy's moving cakes were no longer surprising to the class so this boat accident didn't get more than a raised eyebrow.

As she did every week, Queen Bea sliced our cakes into pieces so everyone could taste each other's.

I was still fretting about the shipwreck when Queen Bea began slicing into my man-in-the-moon cake. "Ah,

nice and light and fluffy. A perfect cake, as usual," she said. She lifted a slice out with a cake server and put it onto Val's plate.

Suddenly Val's eyes got wide and startled.

On the center of Val's plate was a beautiful golden yellow slice of vanilla cake with green buttercream frosting and sparkling sugar crystals. And sticking up from the center of the sliver was a long, brown, fuzzy tail.

Chapter Five

THE SECRET RECIPE

Val screeched. I yelped. Kathleen gagged. Queen Bea took the dish, poked the slice of cake with a fork, then tugged on the tail with her thumb and pointer finger. Out came a small plastic mouse wearing a blue bow tie.

"What have we here?" she said, grinning from ear to ear.

"Sadie strikes again," I muttered*. I suspected Sadie had accidentally juggled two of her plastic mice right into my cake tins yesterday, where they had sunk into the batter only to be found today in front of my whole class. *Ugh!*

"Well, that takes the cake!" snorted Mr. Hiro.

"Where's Mrs. Mouse?" asked Kathleen. "We'd better send out a rescue team."

"Some say the moon is made of green cheese," joked Karlin, "and you know how mice love cheese."

My face felt as hot as a flame and I figured it was as red as one too.

Later on, Queen Bea said she wanted to tell us something important. “Just about everything I learned about baking I learned from my mother. Eating her cake was like listening to your favorite song. You just didn’t want it to end.

“Besides being a talented baker, my mother was also an animal lover. Way back when, she helped build the first building for the Daisy Brook Animal Shelter. She sawed wood and hammered nails and painted. If she was still alive, I know she’d be helping with the new building. But I figured out a way she *can* help.

“You know my secret cake recipe?” she continued. “It’s my mother’s. I know she’d be tickled if it was included in the cookbook that helps raise money for all the cats, dogs and other animals waiting to be adopted.”

We couldn’t believe our ears. The secret recipe in our cookbook? This was huge.

“How about a sneak peek for your favorite

students?" teased Mr. Hiro.

"No sirree, it must be top-secret until the book comes out," Queen Bea said. "If the secret ingredient is revealed ahead of time, there'd be no reason to buy the book. We want to sell lots of cookbooks, right?"

We three-way pinky promised* that we wouldn't look at the recipe.

Queen Bea handed me a piece of paper towel folded in half. "All I had to jot the recipe on was a paper towel," she said with a chuckle. "Do you know that's the first time I've ever actually written down the recipe? I usually keep it right up here." She tapped her pointer finger on the side of her forehead.

I quickly tucked the recipe inside the doors of Cupcake Corner while we cleaned up the cake (and mice).

While we were putting the decorations away, everyone chatted about Queen Bea's trip. She told us she was taking a train to Coco Springs, riding a bus to Fernwood Cove, then a ferry to Merry Island where she'd hop on a bicycle and pedal the rest of

the way to her son's cabin on Bluebird Lane.

When Mr. Hiro learned that Queen Bea was leaving on Saturday, he said that happened to be the day he was the engineer on the same route.

"I'll give you a tour of the engine," he promised Queen Bea.

Was he trying to butter Queen Bea up in hopes of getting the recipe?* I wondered.

Val seemed unusually quiet. I asked her about the upcoming trip to her friend's cottage, but I could see she didn't want to have a conversation.

Karlin said that he was getting plenty of cake orders at the Rock & Roll Bowling Alley. "They *look* good, but honestly, they don't *taste* that hot and they're crumbly. Yours always turn out just right, Jenny. Would you be interested in making bowling pin cakes for us?"

"Absolutely," Lucy piped up. She handed him an order form and he was still filling it out when my mom picked me up.

"Mom," I complained as we walked to the car, "Sadie ruined my cake."

"It was an accident," pouted Sadie. "Besides, I'm just a little kid."

"Well, I must admit it was sort of funny," I said.

"Not funny! My poor mice," wailed Sadie, "trapped in a cake overnight. They must have been so scared." She shuddered* as she picked the crumbs out of Mrs. Mouse's ear, who had been rescued from under the man-in-the-moon's smile. "All better?" she whispered tenderly in Mrs. Mouse's ear.

Chapter Six

DOUBLE TROUBLE

A boom of thunder and flash of lightning woke me up on Saturday morning. I cuddled in bed with Snuggles for a few minutes and thought about a Halloween cake that had been floating around in my imagination.

I wanted to make a pumpkin-shaped cake, but couldn't quite figure out how to do it. Finally my brain woke up and I found the solution.

I'd make two Bundt® cakes (which are made in a round, grooved pan with a hole in the center). Once they'd cooled, I'd turn one upside down, frost the top and put the other cake on top of it. That would make it round like a pumpkin. Orange frosting and a brownish-green stem would be the finishing touches. I couldn't wait to try it.

All that thinking about cake made my stomach growl. *Oatmeal with chopped apples sprinkled with cinnamon sounds good,* I thought.

It was a little chilly, so I wrapped my cozy bathrobe

over my favorite pink-and-white pajamas and put on my comfy slippers. Yawning, I stretched my arms up to the ceiling. Snuggles yawned, too, then followed me downstairs to the kitchen.

My mom was in the breakfast nook reading the paper and sipping a cup of tea. "I just got a message that your soccer game against the Wildcats was cancelled today and rescheduled for next Saturday. This storm is supposed to last all day."

It was disappointing news, because if we had won this game, we'd take first place in our league. But then again, now I could try out the pumpkin cake.

First I checked Lucy's list. Business was booming!

This Week's Cupcake Corner Delivery

24 Pink Cupcakes with Pink Frosting for Val's Mom

36 Ladybug & Flower Cupcakes for the Garden Club

6 Smiley Face Cupcakes

6 Butterfly Cupcakes

6 Rooster Cupcakes

2 Crazy Cakes

1 Kitty-Cat and 1 Monkey Cake for the Dobb Twins' Party (they're turning Two!)

2 Bowling Pin Cakes for the Rock & Roll Bowling Alley

1 Pumpkin Cake

To make the job a little easier, I decided to bake all 78 cupcakes using one of my most popular recipes: Strawberry Chocolate Chip. Then I'd decorate the tops. I checked Sketchpad #2 to jog my memory about the designs.

The Painting Party cupcakes would be decorated with a tall swirl (almost like an ice cream cone) of bubble-gum pink frosting. The Garden Club's cupcakes had charming ladybugs and bright daisies on top.

I'd decorate the butterfly cupcakes with swirling frosting wings and black licorice laces for the antennae*. The rooster cupcakes would be adorable with candy corn beaks, black candy eyes, and a comb* made of fruit leather that was cut into three tiny triangles.

The crazy cakes were decorated with polka dots, stripes, and diamonds in bright colors. The kitty-cat and monkey cake designs were as cute as can be. And the bowling pins were frosted white with two bright red stripes around the "necks."

I washed my hands, put on my pink apron and got out everything I needed: recipes, ingredients, mixing bowls, a whisk, wooden spoons, measuring cups and spoons, spatula, mixer and beaters.

My assistant (my mom) heated up the oven. We greased and floured cake pans so the cake wouldn't stick and put the paper liners in the cupcake trays. We carefully measured each ingredient, mixed batter and poured it into the pans and trays. Then my mom placed everything in the oven and I set the timer.

The juggler in our family had a play date until after lunch, so there was no fear of little critters jumping into the batter.

The first two trays of cupcakes went into the oven and soon the wonderfully sweet smell of strawberries and sugar filled the kitchen. I turned on the oven light and peeked in the window. They were rising just right.

When all the cupcakes were baked to perfection, my mom took them out of the oven. I put on my oven mitts and moved them onto the white metal

baker's rack in the pantry to cool.

After lunch it was time to mix the frosting. I laughed out loud thinking about how Lucy had put the frosting on her cake before baking it. My mom asked me what was so funny and I told her the story. She thought that was hilarious, too.

By two o'clock the baker's rack was filled with creative cakes on stands and colorful cupcakes in cupcake trees and on platters.

My mom and I stood back and admired our work. They all looked delicious.

R-i-n-g, r-i-n-g! R-i-n-g, r-i-n-g!

It was Lucy on the phone. "Too bad about the soccer game," she said. "My mom said as long as it's going to rain all day, she'll start typing the recipes for the cookbook into the computer. Can I come over and get the purple sneaker box?"

"Oh gee," I said, "we brought it back to Cupcake Corner, remember?"

My mom suggested that we drive to Cupcake Corner before we picked up Sadie from her play date. I told Lucy we'd drop it off at her house

later and she reminded me not to forget the secret recipe.

"My mom will type that last," she said. "She promised that she'll keep the ingredients top-secret. She won't even let me see the recipe."

As we dashed down the sidewalk to The Sweet Shoppe, there was a huge downpour and it was so windy that our umbrellas flipped inside out.

Mr. Figg struck up a conversation with my mom and they chatted while I went to get the purple box. As I pulled it from the cupboard, I realized how heavy it was. There must have been fifty or sixty recipes in there.

Typing them was going to be quite a chore for Lucy's mom. I decided I'd bake her a lemon cake (her favorite flavor) decorated with a bundle of frosting sunflowers (her favorite flower) that said, "Thanks a Bunch!"

I smiled thinking about our cookbook, which Lucy and I had decided to name *Top-Secret & Scrumptious Desserts*. The kids at school were excited that their families' recipes would appear

in our book. With the secret recipe in it, my mom predicted we'd sell oodles* of copies and raise a lot of money. People were already calling to see when the book would be ready for sale.

That reminded me I needed to get the recipe. *Whatever you do, don't look at it,* I told myself.

But I didn't have to worry about that—because it was GONE! I searched the cabinet, I looked in the purple box, and I looked all around and behind the cabinet.

Oh my goodness, what am I going to do now? I thought. *Everyone is counting on that recipe to sell lots of cookbooks.*

I know, I thought, *I'll call Queen Bea!*

Then I remembered: Queen Bea had already left for her one-month vacation. The cookbook would be going to the printer in three weeks. And there was no phone where she had gone so I couldn't reach her.

First the sketchpad had suspiciously* disappeared. Now the very important secret recipe was stolen. Was someone trying to sabotage* the cookbook? Did that someone want Cupcake Corner to fail?

Chapter Seven

CUPCAKES & STOMACHACHES

That night I tossed and turned. I woke up around midnight and worried about what could have happened to the recipe and who might have wanted it badly enough to steal it.

There were lots of people who wanted that recipe. But no one knew that I put it in the cupboard at Cupcake Corner.

That's not true, I thought. *Everyone in my cake decorating class saw me put the recipe there. Did one of them nab it?*

Was it Karlin, whose cakes were too crumbly? Maybe he thought if he had the secret recipe his baking would improve and he'd be able to make the bowling cakes himself. Then he could keep all the money. I'd read enough mystery books to know that money is often a motive* for crime.

Or perhaps it was Val, who seemed jealous that

her mom had asked me to make cupcakes for the Painting Party. Getting even with someone (revenge) is another popular motive with lawbreakers.

And what about Mr. Hiro? He was certainly determined to get that recipe! He'd asked Queen Bea for the recipe at three classes in a row. Maybe he figured that if she wouldn't give it to him, he'd take it.

Once Lucy's mom had finished typing the last of the students' recipes, I'd have to either hand over the secret recipe or confess what had happened.

A shadow from a branch moved up and down on my wall. The pipes in our old house clanged*. Snuggles purred. It seemed like forever before I drifted back to sleep.

The next morning Lucy and her dad came by for the cakes and cupcakes so they could deliver them to The Sweet Shoppe.

Even though people usually picked up their orders at The Sweet Shoppe, Lucy had volunteered to deliver the Painting Party cupcakes to Val's house. The guests were arriving at noon and Val's mom was going to be busy getting ready.

Lucy hadn't asked about the secret recipe yet, and I didn't have the courage to tell her. She oohed and aahed when she saw the pink cupcakes.

I took a plate from the pantry containing eight pink cupcakes. "I made too many. Would you like a sample from Cupcake Corner?"

Uncle Bob's eyes lit up. He took one and ate it in three bites. "Out of this world," he said, licking pink frosting from the corner of his mouth. "But I might need to sample one more just to make sure." He said the second was even better than the first.

As Uncle Bob backed his car out of our driveway, Lucy hollered out the window, "The twins are going to love the kitty and monkey birthday cakes!"

I was happy all day thinking that our desserts were going to be part of two special celebrations today and one tomorrow.

That warm fuzzy feeling didn't last long. The next day after school there was a knock knock-knock-knock-knock, knock knock on the door. *Oh good, that's Lucy,* I thought.

She was on the doorstep and out of breath from running up the driveway. Her face was red and her frown told me that she'd figured out the secret recipe was missing.

"Lucy, I meant to tell you—" I started.

She interrupted, "You *know*? How could you know that the Garden Club just called and cancelled our big order for the ladybug and flower cupcakes?"

"Are you serious?!" I exclaimed. "They cancelled our order? Why?"

Lucy threw her hands up in the air. "I don't know, Jenny. It was weird. They left a message on our phone that said thank you very much but they were sorry they didn't need the cupcakes anymore. They said we could keep the money they paid."

I groaned and tried to come up with an explanation. Snuggles circled around my legs and

sat still. He tilted his head to one side like he was as puzzled as we were.

R-i-n-g, r-i-n-g! R-i-n-g, r-i-n-g!

My mom picked up the phone. "Hello, Mr. Figg. How are things at The Sweet Shoppe today?" Then, "Oh, I see…yes, that's odd…okay, thanks for calling. Bye."

"Girls," my mom said, with disappointment on her face, "that was Mr. Figg. I'm afraid he called to let you know there are still plenty of baked goods

left at Cupcake Corner, so you don't need to bake on Wednesday."

"Don't they need more cupcakes?" I asked.

"I guess not. Three sold on Sunday and none since," she said gently.

I started to panic*. "What about the crazy cakes and the pumpkin cake?"

"Honey, I'm sure they'll sell tomorrow," she said, patting me on the shoulder.

A pat on the shoulder meant she felt sorry for me. I felt sorry for me, too.

"I don't understand," said Lucy. "Business was tiptop until yesterday."

"What are we going to do with the Garden Club's cupcakes?" I cried. "They'll go to waste."

In her usual manner, Lucy looked on the bright side. "Go to waste? No way. They're too sweet and tasty. Let's bring a dozen to the fire station. That was so fun when they came to our school last week and let us go on Engine #2. The cupcakes can be a thank you to the firefighters."

I caught on to her thinking "Good idea. And

how about the police station? We can bring a dozen there, too."

My mom added, "We're going to Grandma's senior center for bingo today, so let's bring a dozen with us. They'll be gone in no time."

And they were. By the time Sadie and my dad yelled "Bingo!" not a crumb was left on the platter.

❧ ❧

"Just tell me, Lucy," I begged at recess. Her swing was moving forward while mine was going back. I pumped harder to catch up with her so I could see her face better. "What are you hemming* and hawing about?"

"Um…it's just that…uggh!" she groaned. "You're *not* going to like this…."

"Spit it out. C'mon, Lucy," I said. She had told me that she heard something awful when she was at the grocery store. I wanted to know but I was also afraid to hear what she had to say. "It can't be *that* bad…can it?"

"OK," she said. "I was behind these two women

in the check-out line and they were talking. Ms. 'A' was holding a package of cupcakes and she said she had been getting cupcakes at Cupcake Corner. My ears perked right up when I heard that.

"But, Ms. 'A' told Ms. 'B' she'd never buy anything there again because she heard that they gave everyone an awful stomachache at a party last weekend."

"A stomachache!" I was shocked. "That's crazy! We ate the exact same cupcakes and we're just fine."

"I know, I know," Lucy said, shaking her head.

"What a horrible, nasty, terrible lie." Heartsick, I put my hands over my face.

"I don't think she was trying to be mean," she said. "That's the story she heard, so she told someone else.

"There's one more thing I think you should know. Val wasn't away last weekend. I saw her looking out the window when we delivered the Painting Party cupcakes. I only saw her for a second, but she didn't look very happy."

"I don't get it," I said. "If she was going to be home, why didn't her mom ask her to make the cupcakes? She must be furious with us.

"What are we going to do about the rumor*?" I moaned. "It will ruin our business."

"Jenny," Lucy said sadly, "I think it already has."

Chapter Eight

BETTER OR BITTER?

A few days later Sadie burst into the kitchen with Sketchbook #2 in her hands. "Jenny, I have a fantabulous idea for a cake. Will you draw it for me? It's a Pirate Treasure Chest Cake."

She looked so excited, I agreed, although I knew it wouldn't sell. In fact, only three cupcakes and one crazy cake had sold lately. And there wasn't one new order.

We still stocked Cupcake Corner with platters of cupcakes and decorated cakes on fancy stands, but mostly they just sat there in the antique display case looking pretty. Lucy's dad was more than happy to eat anything that didn't sell. Uncle Bob said he couldn't decide which cupcakes he'd liked better, the German Chocolate, Carrot, or Apple Spice.

I flipped through the pages of the sketchpad. I'd been so discouraged about the rumor, I hadn't opened it in a few days. Why bother?

As Sadie described her Pirate Treasure Chest Cake, I drew every itty-bitty detail: an old-fashioned lock made of yellow frosting, golden candy coins and a pearl necklace of white gumballs draping out from under the lid.

When the sketch was done, she jumped around excitedly.

"Maybe I could be a partner," she said. "Now that I'm a big kid I can be a *big* help."

"I'll make the cake," I said, "but I already have a partner, Sadie. I'll tell you what. If it turns out good, maybe it could go on the front cover of the cookbook."

"All right!" she cried and skipped away merrily with her ark under her arm.

I really enjoyed drawing again. *Even if there aren't any new orders, I can still draw, right?* I asked myself. *I can still have fun coming up with new designs.*

It certainly seemed like someone wanted Cupcake Corner to go out of business. Was it the same person who swiped my sketchpad, stole the recipe and started the rumor?

I had thought about saying very sweetly to Val, "How did your mother's Painting Party go?" and maybe I'd get some information. But Val hadn't been to school for a few days. If she started the

rumor, was she feeling too guilty to face us?

Lucy still had no idea about the missing secret recipe. Not telling her the truth felt like lying.

After all, she was counting on that recipe to sell books and so were all the people who were helping with the *Top-Secret & Scrumptious Desserts* cookbook.

A lot of classmates had signed up to be on teams for The Baking Bonanza. Lucy's mom was almost finished typing all the recipes and The Sweet Shoppe offered to let us use their kitchen in the back. A local grocery store was kind enough to donate all the ingredients and a printer had volunteered to make our book for the cost of the paper. That way we could raise even more money for the shelter.

It was time to tell Lucy the truth. I called her and broke the news.

I should have known that Lucy wouldn't be mad. She tried to make me feel better. "We have lots of awesome recipes, so it's still going to be a fantastic book," she said.

I hung up and was in the middle of a long sigh

when the phone rang. It was the chief of the fire department.

"Thank you for the ladybug cupcakes you and Lucy brought over," he said. "They were such a huge hit, they were gone before I even had a chance to get down the pole!

"Everyone here thought they were fantastic. So we have a question to ask you. Could you make 36 cupcakes for the Community Pride Festival next weekend?"

The Community Pride Festival has been held in our town for the last 27 years. It was a celebration of all the things that make Little Falls special. Plus there are bands, dancers, a rock climbing wall and a magic show.

The chief continued, "We're going to have a booth at the festival that teaches people about fire safety. If we had cupcakes, we might get more people to come to our booth. And that means more people who will learn about how to make their homes safer."

I was thrilled and told him so. I suggested that the cupcakes be decorated to look like their firehouse

dog, Martha May, who is white with floppy brown ears and a cute brown circle around her right eye. He thought that was a terrific idea. I told him Lucy would drop off an order form.

I hung up the phone. Hooray! *Once people taste these cupcakes, they'll know the rumor is a lie,* I thought. *I'll start practicing the design now so they are perfect for next weekend.*

A couple of my cake-decorating books were in the cupboard at Cupcake Corner, so I asked my mom if we

could go to The Sweet Shoppe.

She said that we could go as soon as Sadie put the animals back into the ark.

I decided to help Sadie and speed things up. Her playroom was a complete mess. "It looks like a tornado hit this place," I teased.

"Stop picking on me," she cried. "I'm just a little kid and little kids make big messes. Mom said so."

She needed a nap and was just being cranky. I began humming a song and tossing her stuffed animals into bins where they belonged. She hummed along and finally we had all the little animals safely in the ark and started off to get my books.

As we were walking down the sidewalk, I saw one of Lucy's yellow posters in a window. My heart stopped. Someone had changed the "e" in "better" to an "i." The poster now read:

DELICIOUS JUST GOT BITTER
AT CUPCAKE CORNER
Buy creative cakes and cupcakes
at The Sweet Shoppe today
or place your order for a party.

On Saturday, everyone was psyched up for the soccer game against the Wildcats. It was our chance to be the #1 champs. We looked like pros in our blue and white uniforms and warm-up jackets.

Our coach had told us to drink plenty of water, eat a healthy dinner and go to bed early on Friday night.

I did go to bed early, but couldn't get to sleep. I was still fuming* about the poster. And I was even more determined to make the cupcakes for the fire department super-duper ultra-wonderful, the best ever.

They were going to be so delicious, we'd be flooded with orders afterwards. Ha! I bet we'd have to turn people away because we'd have too much business. Cupcake Corner would be filled with baked goods of every kind and then sell out within minutes. A line of customers would trail out of the store, onto the sidewalk and around the corner….

That is what I was thinking about when there were just forty-two seconds left in the game and the score was tied. And that's what I was thinking when my teammate passed the ball to me, when it went right between my legs, and when it scored the winning goal—*for the other team.*

Oh. My. Goodness. I will never ever in a million years live this down. And the worst part was that Val was on the Wildcats' team.

The Wildcats whooped and jumped into the air and high-fived each other. I looked on glumly as they thumped one another on the back and hugged. They raised their fists chanting, "Wild-cats-rule! Wild-cats-rule! Wild-cats-rule!"

Lucy put her arm around my shoulder and walked off the field with me.

As we trudged to the bench, I remembered the

time she asked me what I thought of her mountain of a cake, which was quite obviously a flop*.

I managed a joke. "What did you think of my goal?"

She smiled and leaned her head in to touch mine. "Oh, Jenny, it was, it was...*really something*!"

Chapter Nine

LOST & FOUND

"Molly Martin's mother asked me to give this to you," my mom said, handing me a brown paper grocery bag.

I'd just baked the dog cupcakes. The kitchen counter where I was standing was covered with drips of water and chocolate batter and smears of cooking oil, so I brought the bag over to the kitchen table to open it.

"Sketchpad #1!" I hurrahed. "How did Molly Martin's mom get this?"

"I guess Molly came into your classroom during recess to get extra help from your teacher on math homework. She put her books down on your desk, then when she went to pick them up, she scooped up your sketchpad by mistake with her things.

"It's been sitting in her backpack, which her mom said is so messy, you couldn't find a refrigerator in there."

I took off my pink apron, washed my hands and called Lucy to fill her in. "So the disappearance of the sketchpad wasn't the work of a thief after all. But what about the secret recipe? And who vandalized* your posters?"

"It's a complete mystery why someone would want to do this," she said. "We might never find out. Let's just focus on the good stuff, like the cupcake order for the fire station and getting the missing sketchpad back. That's great timing because now we can put some of those drawings in the cookbook."

"You're right," I said. "As soon as my chocolate cupcakes are cool, I'm going to practice the dog decorations. I'll bring one over when they're done."

"Oh goody," Lucy said. "That's one of the reasons I love being your partner."

Drumming my fingers on the kitchen table, I thought about the cutest way to decorate the puppy dog cupcakes. I knew just what to do. I looked at the kitchen and thought, *Ugh! I'll deal with this mess later.*

The dog's hair would be vanilla frosting, with a little chocolate frosting mixed in for the ears and the circle around the eye. The tastiest recipe for vanilla frosting was

on page 33 of my *Fifty Ways to Make Fantastic Frosting Workbook*, which I had brought home from The Sweet Shoppe the other day.

I pulled the book from my yellow Li'l Chef tote bag. As I flipped through the pages, a paper towel fluttered out of the book. The secret recipe! *Hooray!* In a split second it landed on the gloppy, oily kitchen counter. *Help!*

I made a grab for it but it had already turned into a soggy pile of mush. Only a piece on the very top of the paper towel hadn't gotten soaked and fallen apart. But even that was spotty and blurred.

I completely forgot that I wasn't supposed to read the top-secret ingredient—but I couldn't even if I wanted to.

Chapter Ten

THE PUZZLING INGREDIENT

"Jenny and Lucy," shouted the chief of the fire department. He was waving us over to the fire safety booth at the Community Pride Festival. The firefighters had brought Engine #5 so the kids could climb in and around it.

As we walked toward him, I saw there was a large crowd of girls from my school gathered at the booth. I recognized a few of the firefighters who had come to our school and taught us about the importance of smoke detectors, being safe in the kitchen and what to do in case of a fire.

"Come and meet your fans," he grinned. "They like your puppy dog cupcakes so much, they asked for seconds."

"You made these cupcakes?" one of the girls asked in a not very nice tone.

I nodded and then noticed a couple of the kids gave each other surprised looks. One girl seemed worried. Another girl scrunched up her face.

When the group had drifted away from the booth, I whispered to Lucy. "That was kind of weird."

"Sure was," Lucy shrugged. "Let's go donate our money for the animal shelter."

We had brought the "Coins for a Cause" Jar from The Sweet Shoppe with us. Even though business was slow lately, the kitty jar was still more than half-full with coins and dollar bills. Ms. Perkins, who runs the animal shelter, was in the booth. Lucy and I had met Ms. Perkins last summer when we volunteered to pet and walk the dogs.

Ms. Perkins was thrilled with the donation and said it would be put to good use for the new building.

It was surprising to see Val volunteering in the booth. She was putting together a display board with pictures of pets that were waiting to be adopted. The board was almost the size of Val. It kept falling over and some of the photos became unstuck.

"Do you need help?" I asked. She said she certainly did. Lucy joined in and so did a few of Val's friends who had been at the fire safety booth. As we all worked together to tape the photos onto the boards, we started talking.

Community Pride
Festival
Face Painting
Adopt a Best Friend
Daisy Brook
ANIMAL SHELTER
COTTON CANDY
FD

I found out a lot of things I didn't know about Val. For example, she's a volunteer at the shelter, too. And she also has a little sister. Val said she couldn't help laughing at Sadie at cake decorating class because Sadie reminds her so much of her sister.

Val has a real soft spot for animals (like me) and she has allergies to some kinds of plants (like me).

"My allergies kicked in on the day of our last cake decorating class," Val said. "When you were talking to me, I felt just awful. By the time the weekend of the Painting Party rolled around, my head was all stuffed up and I felt so lousy I couldn't even go away to my friend's cottage.

"The only good part," she continued, "was that I was able to sneak one of your pink cupcakes before the party began. The bittersweet chocolate chips made them delicious. They were so good I ate five!"

I hooted with laughter. "Oh my gosh, you must have gotten a terrible stomachache."

"Did I ever!" she said.

That was the moment the mystery of the cupcake rumor unraveled like a ball of yarn.

Her friend Suzanne looked puzzled, "Val, I thought you said Jenny used bitter chocolate and you got a stomachache."

Then Nancy said to Suzanne, "Uh-oh, I thought you told me Jenny's cupcakes *were bitter* and they gave her a stomachache."

Then Ann said to Nancy, "Oops, my dog was barking like crazy while we were talking on the phone and maybe I didn't get the story right. It sounded like you said the cupcakes were *so bitter everyone got a stomachache.*"

And Pam said to Ann, "That's what I thought you told me, too. After I told my mom, I think she might have warned her Garden Club to steer clear of Cupcake Corner because their cupcakes made everyone at the party sick. I'm so sorry!"

And Kathy, Amy and Maddy said to Pam, "And that's why our moms won't let us go to Cupcake Corner after school…"

It all became crystal clear. I joked, "No wonder you all looked worried when you heard I made the

puppy dog cupcakes."

Lucy added, "And *that's* why somebody changed the sign to 'bitter.'"

That started Lucy giggling. "This is like the Telephone Game we used to play. Remember? One person whispers a message into someone's ear, who whispers it to another person, and so on. After a few people, the message is completely different from what it started out as."

Her giggling turned into uncontrollable fits of laughter. And it must have been catching, because I started laughing. Then everybody started. Pretty soon tears were rolling down our cheeks.

Ms. Perkins came over and looked pleased. "See? It's just like I always say: volunteering is a lot of fun."

Lucy, the best organizer I know, used the happy mood at the animal shelter's booth to round up more volunteers for The Baking Bonanza.

We also decided as a group to start a *good* rumor about Cupcake Corner. Instead of the news getting worse and worse, we'd make it *better* and *better*.

Before long, the whole town would be coming to Cupcake Corner for our desserts.

What a great day it had been. There was only one thing that could make it the best day ever. And that was figuring out what the secret ingredient under the gloppy smudges was.

That night I flopped into the armchair and studied the messy bit of paper towel that Queen Bea had written the recipe on. Lucy had tried to guess what the ingredient was earlier but without any luck.

I looked at the name of the cake recipe. "Mom's Secret (Glob Glob) Fizz Cake." I had three clues to work with:

1) The secret ingredient was in the name of the recipe.
2) The secret ingredient looked like it was two words:

R __ __ T   B __ __ R

3) The recipe had to do with something fizzy.

I was deep in thought when I heard Sadie dump all the animals out of the ark. She began marching them across the floor and up my leg.

"Sadie, I'm trying to think," I said.

"Wouldn't you rather play with us?" She looked at

me with her sweet brown eyes as the animals galloped across my knee. "The kangaroos and skunks have asked you and me to come over. That's really special Jenny, because you have to be a princess, a giraffe or a big kid to be invited to their house for root beer floats."

"Maybe later—" I stopped in the middle of my thought. "Did you say 'root beer'? Oh my gosh, Sadie, you're a genius!" She had no idea what I was talking about, but was happy to celebrate anyway. I took both of her hands in mine and we twirled and chanted "*Root* beer, *root* beer, *root* beer, *root* beer" until we were dizzy and seeing stars.

Once we caught our breath, Sadie put a glittering princess crown on my head and a sparkly pink cape around my shoulders. We sat at her little play table and sipped from make-believe cups.

I nodded to the kangaroos and skunks who were sharing one chair, smiled at the stuffed giraffe who was sitting on his own chair, and winked at Sadie. "This has been a delightful party," I said to all the guests as I patted my tummy. "That root beer hit* the spot."

Chapter Eleven

THE BAKING BONANZA

While Queen Bea was on vacation, *Baking Today* magazine came to the island to interview her about the cookbook she was working on. They took photos of her making a Peach Dream Pie over a campfire and asked her why she decided to write a book about campfire baking.

"One year on a vacation, my mother taught me to bake on a wood stove," she explained. "She was so talented, I bet she could have cooked over a candle flame.

"Her most famous recipe has always been a family secret," she told the magazine, "until next month that is. That's when it will be featured in a new cookbook, *Top-Secret & Scrumptious Desserts*."

She told them all about how the Little Falls Elementary School was donating the profits to the

animal shelter.

Even though the article hadn't even appeared in the magazine, word about the secret recipe spread instantly. The animal shelter was flooded with phone calls. Bookstores across the country wanted to sell our books. The Sweet Shoppe had people lined up out the door and around the corner to pre-order* copies.

When the company that published* Queen Bea's other cookbooks heard about the secret recipe, they took a boat to the island to talk to her.

Then a woman and man in fancy suits made a special trip to Little Falls. They met with Ms. Perkins from the animal shelter, the two partners of Cupcake Corner (Lucy and me), our parents and Queen Bea (who came back early from her vacation just for the meeting).

They said if we agreed, they would print the books and sell them in stores around the country. In return they would pay for half the cost of the new building for the animal shelter!

"That's just fine," said Queen Bea, "because I also have my mother's secret *pie* recipe that would be perfect for a cookbook sequel*. We can call it *Even More Top-Secret & Scrumptious Desserts*. Would you agree to print that one, too? That would pay for the other half of the animal shelter's building."

They agreed. Our parents and Queen Bea signed the legal papers. And we had ourselves a deal.

After everyone had left, Queen Bea pulled two boxes out of a bag. They were wrapped in silver paper with glittery purple curling ribbons. She gave one to Lucy and one to me. "These are from me to you," she said, "for The Baking Bonanza."

The gift tag on my box read "To Queen Jenny" and Lucy's read "To Queen Lucy." We ripped off the shimmering paper and opened the boxes. I pulled out a white chef's hat, put it on and winked at Lucy, who was already wearing hers too. Under layers of tissue paper, we found another surprise—white baker's jackets.

Edna Bea

Chapter Twelve

THE TASTE OF SUCCESS

The Baking Bonanza was a blast. Lucy and I wore our baking uniforms. Val, as well as boys and girls from school, and friends old and new, put on aprons. My mom and other parents, including my Uncle Bob (who was there hoping for leftovers), helped out, too.

The Sweet Shoppe had all the tools we needed, including cake and cupcake pans, bowls, spatulas, rolling pins, spoons, mixers, beaters, whisks and more.

Lucy organized everyone into baking teams. She gave one recipe to each team, reading the recipe names aloud as she passed them out.

Some of them had funny old-fashioned names like Shoofly Pie (made with sweet molasses inside and crispy crumbs on top), Blueberry Grunt (fruit with a biscuit topping), Apple Brown Betty (layers of fruit and buttery

bread crumbs) and Soda-Cracker Pie (which tastes like apple pie but is actually made with crackers).

Then Lucy had a pep talk with us and told us the importance of washing our hands and never-ever-ever licking the spoons or our fingers while baking. She said that would be super yucky for people who would be eating the desserts later.

I told everyone that the allergy-free recipes for the cookbook were being baked at our classmate Catherine's house. She, her brother Michael, our friends Nicholas and Bella, and a whole bunch of other friends and their parents were making fifteen desserts there without nuts, eggs and other ingredients that might cause an allergic reaction. I dialed Catherine's number and had everyone on the count of 1-2-3 say hello. They were on speakerphone so everyone could hear them shout a big "Hello!" back to us.

Then Lucy and I said together, "The Baking Bonanza is about to begin! Are you ready?"

Everybody hollered an enthusiastic "Yes!"

Lucy and I shouted, "On your mark, get set, go!"

Then everyone got to work.

All the bakers were measuring and stirring and beating. Some were scooping dollops* of cookie dough onto metal cookie sheets. Others sprinkled candy confetti into batter and poured it into baking pans. Frosting in chocolate and every color of the rainbow was made. Pie dough was rolled and heaped with fresh fruit. The pie crust edges were sealed with a fork and a smiley face was cut into the top crust so steam could escape.

Val was my partner and we had a grand time.

The girl who was supposed to be Lucy's partner was sick that day, so Lucy was on her own to make a Toasted Coconut Coffee Cake. That made me a little worried.

One lip-smacking dessert after another came out of the ovens: melt-in-your-mouth cakes, cookies, pies, cupcakes, muffins, sticky buns, brownies, blondies, snicker doodles, cobblers and whoopee pies.

Catherine, Michael, Nicholas, Bella and their whole baking party called to tell us all their desserts had turned out fantastic.

Everything looked spectacular and smelled just wonderful. *Baking Today* magazine came to take a photo

of The Baking Bonanza and asked if they could bring a cake back to their office. They said it might be shown in the magazine.

"Let's pick the most perfect dessert," I said. *How will I ever choose just one?* I thought.

I heard the oven timer beep and turned to see Lucy lifting her cake onto the counter. There was a twinkle in her eye. "What do you think of my cake, Jenny?"

I was astonished*. It looked like Queen Bea had made it.

"It's *really something*," I said. "No joking, it *really* is."

And to the reporter I said, "This is the cake you'll want to take."

The next day was the groundbreaking ceremony for the Daisy Brook Animal Shelter. A groundbreaking ceremony celebrates the day construction starts for a new building.

Ms. Perkins gave Queen Bea, Lucy and me shiny shovels. A photographer from the local newspaper snapped photos while we dug the first shovelfuls of dirt.

Over a hundred people came from school and from all around Little Falls. Snuggles was there wearing his purple-and-black striped harness and leash. You could tell he thought he was quite stylish and important.

The mayor said a few words, then Ms. Perkins said she wanted to make a special announcement.

"We called Queen Bea's mother 'Mom Bea' because over the years she was a mom to more adopted pets than I could count. She always made sure the animals in our town had a safe, warm place to call home.

"Through her secret recipe, she's still doing that by helping us raise money for the new building. That's why

I'd like to dedicate* the building to her. This will be hung on the outside wall as soon as it's finished." She held up a large brass sign that was engraved with the words:

THIS BUILDING WAS MADE POSSIBLE BY

MOM BEA

I scanned the crowd. I saw Queen Bea's misty eyes and knew they were tears of pure happiness. Sadie was standing right up front next to my mom. She was wearing what she called her "big kid dress" and she was eyeing the tables jam-packed with mouthwatering desserts from The Baking Bonanza.

There was also a table of delicious desserts that were allergy-free, a table holding cups of water, and another table with pictures of pets who were waiting to be adopted.

Lucy had a clipboard with a volunteer sign-up sheet for the next cookbook project. She was ready to organize all of our friends into action.

How sweet it is, I thought. *And speaking of sweet, isn't it about time for a piece of that Shoofly Pie?*

Glossary

*Many words have more than one meaning. Here are the definitions of words marked with this symbol * (an asterisk) as they are used in sentences.*

allergy (allergic): *coughing, sneezing, rash or another reaction that might happen to a person who comes in contact with something he/she is sensitive to*

allergy*-free: *without ingredients that might cause an allergic reaction*

antennae: *feelers on the head of a butterfly*

ark: *a large boat with a flat bottom*

aroma: *a nice smell*

astonished: *very surprised*

blue: *sad*

bonanza: *an event that creates a great amount of something*

boot, as in "got the boot": *forced out, asked to leave*

butter, as in "butter up": *give lots of praise in order to please someone*

clanged: *made a loud sound like metal slamming*

comb: *the red crest on the head of a rooster*

compliment: *words of approval and praise*
dedicate: *build in honor of a special person*
diploma: *a certificate or piece of paper that shows a student has completed a class*
dollops: *blobs of soft food*
double: *twice as much as what is usually used*
dozen: *a group of twelve*
factory: *a building where things are made using machinery*
flop: *a failure*
fuming: *being angry*
fundraising: *raising money for a good cause*
hemming, as in "hemming and hawing": *pausing and not giving an answer right away*
hesitated: *waited or paused*
hit, as in "hit the spot": *satisfied exactly what was wanted*
icing: *a coating for cakes that is like frosting, but thinner*
locomotive: *a vehicle with an engine that pushes or pulls railroad cars on tracks*
motive: *a reason for doing something*
muttered: *spoke in a low voice or grumbled*
oodles: *a great number*
panic: *to feel a sudden wild fear that is not controlled*

pre-order: *order before something is available for sale*
printer: *a business that prints books*
profit: *the amount of money left after subtracting the amount it cost to make something*
published: *made a book ready for sale*
rumor: *a possibly untrue story spread from person to person*
sabotage: *destroy on purpose*
senior, as in "senior center": *a place where elderly or older adults gather for activities, learning and fun*
sequel: *a book that continues a subject started in an earlier book*
shuddered: *shook, trembled*
solar panels: *panels that use the sun's rays to make energy for electricity or heating*
sprawled: *resting with legs and arms spread out in a relaxed way*
suspiciously: *causing distrust*
three-way pinky promised: *three people's pinky fingers hooked together to show a promise has been made*
tickled, as in "tickled pink": *very pleased*
vandalized: *destroyed on purpose*
wilderness: *land that grows naturally, with few or no people living there*

Volunteers are

All it takes is a big ♥
and a little time.

You can make a big difference by volunteering.
A volunteer is someone who freely gives their time to help out.
Giving to others actually gives you something back—it feels great!

There are lots of places that could use a kind and energetic person like you. Think about what interests you. Do you like working with people, animals, younger children, senior citizens or for the environment? Ask your parent to help you do a little research on the computer about volunteering. Better yet, ask them to volunteer with you. Check out books on volunteering opportunities at your local library and look in the local newspaper.

Volunteering not only helps the community, it's fun and a great way to meet new friends. Get your classmates, Girl Scout troop, club, sports team, neighbors, church, or family involved, too.

Here are a few ideas to get you started:

Organize a Neighborhood Cleanup

Pick a date, make fliers, bring rakes, trash bags, garbage cans, recycling bins and gloves. Just an hour or two is all it will take until you'll see a difference.

Collect Canned Goods for a Food Drive

Imagine providing dinner for families who cannot afford a healthy meal. Food drives help stock pantry shelves for people in need.

Rake Leaves or Shovel Snow for an Elderly Neighbor

You'll instantly feel fantastic knowing you've helped someone out.

Be a Tutor

Are you good in math, reading or science? Offer your skills to help a student who could use extra help. Ask your teacher or principal if they might be able to pair you with another student who needs more practice.

Read at a Senior Center

Help out at a retirement home. Do you have a talent for reading aloud, singing or playing an instrument? The residents might be delighted to hear you perform.

Start a Penny Drive

Pennies add up! Collect coins at your school or church and donate them to a special cause—a children's hospital, the local animal shelter or someone in the community who needs help.

Collect New Socks

Most of us put on socks every morning without even thinking about it. But for homeless people, new socks are a luxury. Begin a sock collection and give comfort to folks who can really use it. Winter hats, scarves, gloves or mittens are also needed at many homeless shelters.

Send "Thank You" Letters

Thank the people who do good work in the community. Send a letter of thanks or bake cupcakes (like Jenny and Lucy did) for the fire department and the police department, or for the postal carrier or librarian.

Collect Dog Treats for Animal Shelters & Food Pantries

Your kindness is sure to bring tail wags from furry four-legged friends.

Sponsor a Soldier

Write letters or send care packages to soldiers who are far from home.

Be Creative!

There are endless ways to raise funds for a cause that's close to your heart. Host a lemonade stand and get a friend to play their violin to attract attention. Sell tickets to a teachers versus parents championship baseball game. Organize a walk around your school's track and ask sponsors to donate money for each lap walked. Put on a play and donate the proceeds. Have a yard sale or bake sale.

Remember, to participate in volunteer work, permission from a parent or adult is required, and volunteer work should always be supervised by your parent or a trusted adult.

Your kindness counts.
Start making a difference today in your community.

About the Author

Susan Cappadonia Love lives in Milton, Massachusetts with her daughter Olivia, who sat on a big boulder next to a pond and brainstormed about this baking story; her daughter Sophie, whom she can always count on for sound opinions; and her husband Scott, who's chockfull of good ideas and can draw a cupcake that looks good enough to eat.

In addition to **The Sweet Shoppe Mystery***, she has also written three other books in the Our Generation® Series,* **The Mystery of the Vanishing Coin, Stars in Your Eyes** *and* **One Smart Cookie***, as well as other children's books.*

Much gratitude goes to Mylene Vallee and Julie Kassabian at Battat Incorporated, whose creativity brings make-believe to life, as well as Alison Morin, Joe Battat, Dany Battat, Batia Tarrab and Gisela Voss.